D0532042

Doggone Feet!

Leslie Helakoski

BOYDS MILLS PRESS

AN IMPRINT OF HIGHLIGHTS

Honesdale, Pennsylvania

To Anders, who always—yes, always—has a place at my table.
And to Desi, who has a place under it.

Text and illustrations copyright © 2013 by Leslie Helakoski
All rights reserved
"Zydeco Shoes" used with permission by the Earl Hebert estate.
For information about permission to reproduce selections from this book,
please contact permissions@highlights.com.

Boyds Mills Press, Inc.
815 Church Street
Honesdale, Pennsylvania 18431
Printed in Mexico
ISBN: 978-1-59078-933-9
Library of Congress Control Number: 2012949018

First edition
The text of this book is set in Montara.

10 9 8 7 6 5 4 3 2 1

I followed Legs home from the park one fine day.

A look with sad eyes and he said I could stay.
We're family now so I help with a chore:
Sit under the table and clean up the floor.

BUT SOMETIMES . . .

YES, SOMETIMES . . .

Legs' fingers will stick,
and I'll clean up those hands with a good thorough lick.

Just me and two feet.

Months later, new feet have arrived on the scene.
They curl next to Legs, so I squeeze in between.

I DON'T LIKE THESE FEET!

These feet without shoes!
They're twirling leg twisters, toe-tapping kiss-kissers,
rule-listing insisters of doggy shampoos.

BUT SOMETIMES...

YES, SOMETIMES...

Those Toes scratch my back.
They dig in my fur till my bones are all slack.

I guess there is room for four feet.

A year passes by and more feet hang above,
with tiny Pink Socks that Legs and Toes love.

I DON'T LIKE THESE FEET!

In that tall shiny chair—
they're hacking hic-cuppers, surprising spit-uppers,
full swinging fling-uppers of arms in the air.

BUT SOMETIMES . . .

YES, SOMETIMES . . .

As part of my job, extra work is a must—
Pink Socks is a slob!

I suppose there is room for six feet.

Blue Boots at the table now bang on and on.
They can't leave that seat till their milk is all gone.

I DON'T LIKE THESE FEET!

These Boots pound a beat!
These splitting head-banging, these noisy new-fangling,
won't-drink-their-milk wrangling, doggone little feet!

BUT SOMETIMES . . .

YES, SOMETIMES . . .

I help, and alas!

My tongue reaches down only half of the glass.

I think I can fit in eight feet.

Small feet have appeared wearing green rubber grippers.
They only like veggies and animal slippers.

I DON'T LIKE THESE FEET!

These Slippers hide meat!
They think meat is ewwy and spit it all chewy
in napkins—pit-touiee—and chomp on a beet.

BUT SOMETIMES . . .

YES, SOMETIMES . . .

I'll tend to the meat,
then swallow the napkin (to keep the floor neat).

Okay, I'll make room for ten feet.

On Sundays, more feet clip-clop over to dine.
Their voice hurts my ears and my throat starts to whine.

I DON'T LIKE THESE FEET!

With their high-pitched halloo.
They wake me from sleeping, while pipping and peeping,
not to mention they're sweeping up things I might chew.

BUT SOMETIMES . . .

YES, SOMETIMES . . .

Shoes won't eat her greens,
and down comes a hand holding peas or string beans.

Well . . . maybe, if I try, I can squeeze in twelve feet.

This table is full,
no spaces to spare.
I wash up Legs' hands
with Toes in my hair.
I clean after Socks
and Boots' banging heels;
I swallow whole napkins
when Slippers eats meals.
I eat what Shoes can't.
(I'm not one to judge.)
I try to keep up,
but it's hard!
I can't budge!
My belly hangs lower each day to the floor.

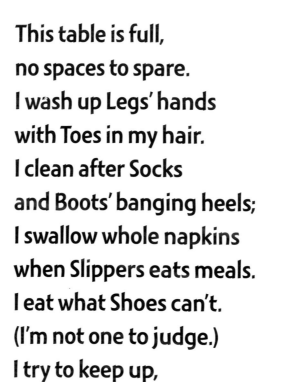

THERE JUST ISN'T ROOM
    FOR
        ONE
            SINGLE
                THING
                    MORE!

New feet at the table—
in fact, quite a few.
For these wee arrivals,
more chairs will not do.
They're fuzzy and soft
and smell oh-so sweet.
Perhaps there is room
for a few tiny feet.

So under the table,
feet scooch on the floor
'cause families

ALWAYS . . .

YES, ALWAYS . . .

MAKE ROOM FOR MORE!